nick jr.

By Mary Tillworth

Based on the teleplay "Sleepover Surprise" by Rachel Vine

Illustrated by Watermark Rights Limited

 A GOLDEN BOOK • NEW YORK

rhcbooks.com
T#: 607387
ISBN 978-0-525-64737-9
Printed in the United States of America
10 9 8 7 6 5 4 3 2 1

Sunny, Blair, and Rox were wearing pajamas for a sleepover night at the salon. After Doodle rolled their sleeping bags out of the closet, they were ready for the slumber party to begin!

Sunny had a special sleepover surprise. She opened a bottle and dabbed a clear liquid onto everyone's hair.

"Are you sure this works?" Rox asked. Their hair didn't look any different.

Sunny smiled. "Oh, it works!" she said. "There's just one more thing to add—the dark!" She asked Doodle to turn off the salon lights.

Rox gasped. “Glow-in-the-dark hair? I can’t believe it!”

“Coolest surprise ever!” squealed Blair.

“Definitely one for the Style Files!” Sunny said with another smile.

Blair checked her schedule to see what was next.

"You made a schedule for a party?" Rox asked. She held up her pillow. "Where on the schedule can I find . . . 'pillow fight'?"

Laughing, the girls bopped each other with their pillows.

After the pillow fight, Blair's tummy rumbled. "Better get back on schedule. Snack time!"

Blair had brought fruit yogurt treats. Rox had a bag of pretzels. Sunny showed everyone a veggie platter she'd made in the shape of the sun.

Doodle chomped on a carrot stick. "My favorite!" he said.

As the girls munched on their snacks, they heard something creak.

Doodle jumped behind Sunny. "Did you hear that?"

"It's coming from outside," said Sunny.

The girls and Doodle followed the sound all the way out to the Glam Van. The back door of the van was open and creaking on its hinges! Sunny closed it.

"See!" she said. "Nothing to fear."

Blair wasn't convinced. "But I shut the door earlier today. I'm sure of it!"

Back in the salon, Blair checked her schedule again. "Teeth brushing is next." She watched as Rox emptied her bag, searching for her toothbrush.

Rox smiled. "I thought I'd brought everything, but I guess not. Do either of you have . . ."

"A spare toothbrush?" Blair handed one to her friend.

After brushing her teeth, Rox turned around to get her hairbrush. She gasped. Everything she had just taken out of her bag was now neatly repacked. Most surprisingly, the carrots from the veggie plate were gone!

“This is getting stranger and stranger,” said Sunny. “Someone is opening the Glam Van door, cleaning up in here, and eating our snacks!”

“The salon is haunted!” said Rox.

“There is an explanation for all this,” Sunny said. “And it’s not ghosts.”

Just to be sure, Blair checked her manicure station. "Nothing," she sighed.

There was a loud crack—but that was just Rox opening a new bag of pretzels.

Then they heard a sound above them.

The girls and Doodle went upstairs to check out the noise. They saw that everything had been tidied up—except for Sunny's bottle of glow-in-the-dark hair paint. Their mysterious visitor had spilled it all over the floor!

Sunny studied the spill. "Definitely not a ghost."

"How can you be sure?" Blair asked.

Sunny asked Doodle to turn off the lights again. "Because ghosts don't leave little glowing paw prints!" she said.

"We know that whoever did this likes two things—cleaning up messes, and carrots!" said Sunny. "I have a plan to catch the culprit."

"Let's gear up and go!" the friends shouted.

Back on the first floor, the girls made a big pile of brushes, bows, and veggies. Sunny rigged a net above the pile and attached a bell to it.

If their mysterious visitor tried to clean up the mess or eat the treats, the bell would ring and the net would drop!

The trap was set. The girls switched off the lights and hid behind the front desk.

They waited.
And waited.
Then they heard the bell!

They turned on the lights and rushed over to the net. Trapped inside was . . . a bunny!

"That's the ghost?" Doodle barked.

"Cutest ghost I've ever seen!" Sunny said.

"She's adorable!" Blair said. "I wonder how she got in here."

"She must have snuck into the Glam Van," said Sunny, "and then found her way into the salon. Mystery solved!"

The bunny hopped into Rox's arms. She giggled. "I think I'll name you . . . Violet!"

It was time for bed. Everyone got into their sleeping bags. Violet snuggled up with Rox.

"Best slumber party ever!" Sunny said happily as they all drifted off to sleep.